THE LITTLE RED HEN

Illustrated by AMYE ROSENBERG

A GOLDEN BOOK • NEW YORK

Western Publishing Company, Inc., Racine, Wisconsin 53404

ONCE there was a little red hen who found some grain. She thought of the fine wheat that would grow if she planted the grain.

"Who will help me plant this grain?" asked the Little Red Hen.

The Cat, the Rat, and the Dog were relaxing in the sun, sipping tea.

"Not I," meowed the Cat.

"Not I," squeaked the Rat.

"Not I," barked the Dog.

"Then I will do it myself," said the Little Red Hen.

Every day the wheat grew taller and more golden. Soon it was ready to be cut.

"Who will help me cut this wheat?" asked the Little Red Hen.

"Not I," meowed the Cat. "I'm too tired."
"Not I," squeaked the Rat. "I'm too small."
"Not I," barked the Dog. "I'm too busy."

"Then I will do it myself," said the Little Red Hen. She cut the wheat and gathered it into bundles. Then she loaded it into the wheelbarrow. It was hard work.

While the Little Red Hen worked, the Cat yawned. the Rat watched a butterfly, and the Dog slept.

Finally the Little Red Hen was ready to take the wheat to the mill. Slowly she pushed the wheelbarrow down the bumpy hill.

The Cat, the Rat, and the Dog went along to see what would happen next.

When they arrived at the mill, the Little Red Hen asked, "Who will help me grind this wheat into flour?"

"Not I," said the Cat, dusting off a place to sit.
"Not I," said the Rat, opening a book.
"Not I," said the Dog, settling back for another nap.

"Then I will do it myself," said the Little Red Hen.
She put the wheat into the grinder. *Whirr, whirr, whoosh!*
Out came the flour. The Little Red Hen put the flour
into big sacks, and set off for home.

The Cat, the Rat, and the Dog went back home too.

"Who will help me make this flour into bread?" asked the Little Red Hen.

"Not I," said the Cat, the Rat, and the Dog.
"Then I will do it myself," said the Little Red Hen.

When the bread was baked, the Little Red Hen took
it out of the oven. Steam rose from the golden loaf.
It smelled delicious.

"Who will help me eat this bread?" asked the Little Red Hen.

"I will!" meowed the Cat.

"I will!" squeaked the Rat.

"I will!" barked the Dog.

"No you will not!" said the Little Red Hen.
"You did not help me plant the grain. You did not
help me cut the wheat or grind it into flour.
You did not even help me make the flour into bread."

"Oh my," meowed the Cat.
"Oh dear," squeaked the Rat.
"Oh no!" barked the Dog.

"And so you will not help me eat the bread,"
said the Little Red Hen. "I will do it myself."